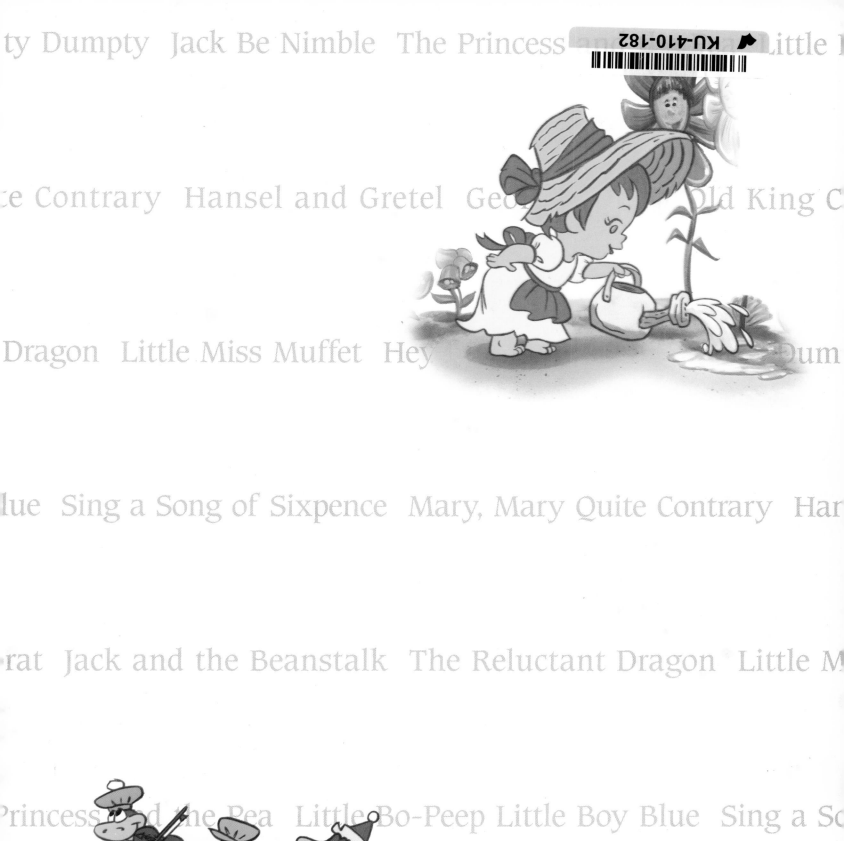

ty Dumpty   Jack Be Nimble   The Princess Little

te Contrary   Hansel and Gretel   Geo   Old King C

Dragon   Little Miss Muffet   Hey   Dum

lue   Sing a Song of Sixpence   Mary, Mary Quite Contrary   Har

rat   Jack and the Beanstalk   The Reluctant Dragon   Little M

Princess d the Pea   Little Bo-Peep Little Boy Blue   Sing a So

Porgy   Old   Dub-Dub   Jack Sprat   Jack and

THE FLINTSTONES®
BEDTIME STORYBOOK

A collection of favourite fairy tales and rhymes
as told by Fred Flintstone to his daughter, Pebbles

Bedrock Press

Atlanta

CONTENTS

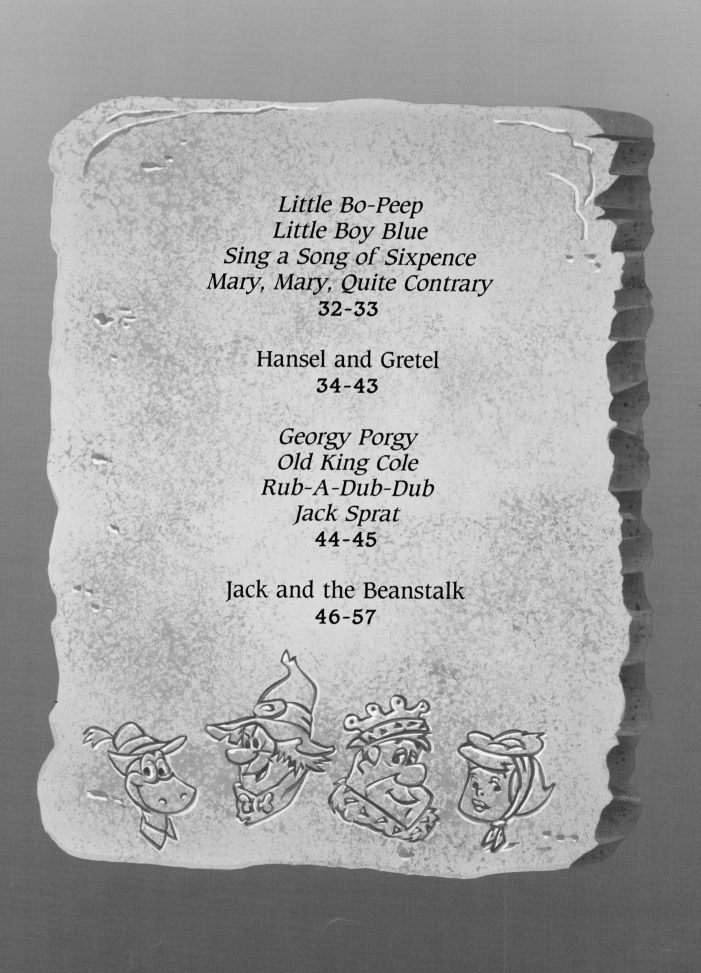

INTRODUCTION

What would you say to a Fairy or Sprite?
Who dances up moonbeans on a cold winter night?
Would you believe that Dragons take flight?
To search for brave Knights with whom they can fight?

Do you know of a Giant who's as big as a house?
Or a Wizard who turns quickly into a mouse?
Are there Witches on broomsticks flying tonight?
Are Trolls under bridges—well out of sight?

Can a bullfrog ever be really a Prince?
Do Leprechauns vanish when put in a pinch?
Are Unicorns always shy, gentle, and wise?
Does a Fox ever dress in human disguise?

If you would know answers to questions like these,
Then just turn the page as fast as you please.
For as sure as wishes and dreams come true,
A fairyland adventure is waiting for you.

THE RELUCTANT DRAGON

nce upon a time, there was a small village tucked
away among the rolling green hills of old England.
And like most little villages it was, for the most part,
a peaceful and quiet place. Not very much of anything ever
happened to cause even a stir of outrage, delight, or just plain curiosity.
That is, until the *dragon* came.

The dragon had taken up residence in a cave on top of a hill overlooking the village. No one knew where the dragon had come from, or how he came to be so near their village. The fact that he was a dragon, and knowing full well what dragons like to do best, sent a shudder of fear through every villager. They imagined the dragon swooping down from his perch on the hill, burning their crops and destroying their homes.

Something would have to be done, and done quickly, before the beast could do his worst.

But indeed, nothing could have been further from this dragon's thoughts. He didn't care a bit for rampaging, pillaging, or plundering. Why the very idea of breathing fire upset him, for it would most certainly lead to a sore throat.

No, this dragon was *different.*

The prospect of bringing pain and misery to anyone was simply beyond this dragon's understanding. He'd much rather smell the sweet spring flowers, enjoy a soothing sunset, or, best of all, write poetry. This dragon adored poetry and spent most of his time reading and writing it!

And to tell the truth, his poems weren't that bad.

But to the villagers down below, he was always the *terrible* dragon. That, since his arrival, he had done nothing wicked or wily, whatsoever, didn't make a bit of difference to them. It was only a matter of time, the townsfolk said, before this beast would begin to behave badly.

So, the elders of the village gathered together to decide what to do about this terrifying beast. They talked, and talked, and talked, until it became quite clear that no one was brave enough to challenge this dragon. Finally, it was decided they would seek the services of the brave knight, Sir George, the Dragonslayer.

This dragon, enjoying the delightful day and reading a bit of verse, spied Sir George in the distance. He thought the knight made a gallant sight on his galloping steed and was considering writing a verse or two about the fellow, when suddenly Sir George crested the hill.

"Ho there, Dragon!" called Sir George.

"Well, ho there to you," replied the dragon.

Sir George cleared his throat, "Dragon! I have come on behalf of . . ."

"Now listen here," interrupted the dragon, "don't hit me, throw stones, squirt water, or do anything of the kind. I won't have it, I tell you! I won't!"

"Hold it, hold it! You are a dragon, are you not?" Sir George cried.

"I most certainly am," replied the dragon.

"Well, then you know why I'm here. So don't give me any trouble." said Sir George.

"If you mean to fight me, fellow, well, you can just forget it," said the dragon. "True, I am a dragon, but I am also a gentleman and I don't care a bit for roughhousing. So, good day, sir!"

Sir George was very surprised, and confused. He had never met a dragon quite like this one.

"But what if I make you fight?" demanded the knight.

"You can't," said the dragon, smiling. "If you try I will simply go into my cave and stay there! You'll soon get quite tired of waiting for me to come out and fight you. And when you do go away, I'll come out again. For, you see, I like it here, and here I will stay!

Sir George thought for a moment.

"I can see you're a respectable fellow," said Sir George. "If it were up to me, I would leave you alone, and that would be that. But the villagers expect a fight. If you don't fight me, they'll just send someone else to take my place. Unless . . ."

"Yes? Unless, what?" asked the dragon, who, by this time, was quite upset with the whole unpleasant business.

"Unless you and I were to have a make-believe battle! You could huff and puff smoke, breathe fire, and generally stamp about while I pretend to attack and defeat you in this little battle of ours. It just might work!"

"If I do this," said the dragon, "you'd be sure to mind where you poke that spear?"

Sir George promised to be careful, and the two shook hands, agreeing to meet in the morning to carry out their plan.

The next day, the entire village arrived for the battle. Sir George appeared upon his mighty steed, lance in hand. But attention was soon drawn to the cave. A thunderous roar bellowed from the opening. The ground began to shake and quake and, in the next moment, the dragon emerged. He stamped about in a frightful rage, as fireballs shot from his mouth and thick smoke blew from his flaring nostrils. He was a terrible sight to behold.

"Boy," thought Sir George, "I hope the dragon remembers our plan."

The two mighty warriors fought throughout the misty morning. However, neither the dragon nor Sir George were really hurt. The dragon did receive a stinging rap to his nose when Sir George came too close with a punch. And Sir George's bottom received a bit of a scorching when the dragon blew a fireball with a little too much might. But, for the most part, neither was the worse for wear.

Finally, the dragon pretended to beg for mercy as he fell in defeat from one of Sir George's blows. Sir George then gave the dragon a good talking-to. The dragon promised never to burn, pillage, plunder, or rampage their village.

No, not ever!

Quite satisfied with the whole affair, the villagers called for a feast in honour of the victorious Sir George—and the defeated dragon.

The banquet was a grand affair that continued long into the starlit night. The dragon told jokes, recited poetry, and impressed the villagers with his well-travelled tales and far-flung adventures. Sir George was very happy to have met *this* dragon. The dragon was never happier, as he now had many new friends. For you see, the dragon, above all, was quite lonely.

But the night was growing old, and it was well past everyone's bedtime.

"Sir George," said the dragon, "would you mind terribly if I asked you to walk me home?"

"Not at all, dragon. Have you forgotten your way?"

"No, no. Not quite," whispered the dragon. "Now, I wouldn't want this to get around, but I'm frightfully afraid of the dark. You understand, my friend, don't you?"

"Yes, yes, come on!" said Sir George, laughing, and the two new friends climbed the hill toward the dragon's home. And throughout the whole valley on that wondrous night, everyone could hear the dragon and Sir George singing a jolly song.

LITTLE MISS MUFFET

Little Miss Muffet
Sat on a tuffet,
Eating her curds and whey.

Along came a spider
Who sat down beside her,
And frightened Miss Muffet away.

HEY DIDDLE, DIDDLE

Hey, diddle, diddle,
The cat and the fiddle,
The cow jumped over the moon;
The little dog laughed
To see such fun,
And the dish ran away with the spoon.

HUMPTY DUMPTY

Humpty Dumpty sat on a wall,
Humpty Dumpty had a great fall.
All the king's horses
And all the king's men
Couldn't put Humpty
Together again.

JACK BE NIMBLE

Jack be nimble,
Jack be quick,
Jack jump over
the candlestick!

THE PRINCESS AND THE PEA

 nce upon a time there was a pretty princess who had to travel a long distance from her father's kingdom. She rode in a royal coach and was accompanied by her royal guard. As she travelled through a neighboring kingdom she saw a beautiful field of flowers.

She called to her coachman to stop, wishing to pick a few flowers and to take a little rest before continuing her journey. Delighted with the bursting blooms, the princess set off into the field with her basket, while her coachman and guards waited. Before long she had wandered quite some distance from the road and well out of sight of her attendants.

Suddenly, without even the whisper of a warning, a terrible storm broke loose from above. Lightning cracked the sky and the ground shook with thunder. The clouds emptied a pounding rain upon the poor princess.

The storm lasted well into night, driving the princess farther and farther away from her royal coach. Before long, she was lost. In the distance, the princess could see a castle sitting upon a hill. She headed for it at once. Finally, as quickly as it had begun, the storm ended. As the sky cleared and the moon shone bright, the princess arrived at the castle.

The princess, her clothes tattered and torn, and her hair and face a mess, knocked on the door. Before long a woman, who was in fact a queen, answered.

"Oh, my dear!" said the queen. "How terrible to be caught in such a storm! It is a wonder you are still alive. Come in, child, come in!" And the queen hurried the poor princess inside.

"I am sorry to bother you," said the princess, "but I was travelling in my father's royal coach and decided to stop for a rest. While picking flowers in a field, I was caught in the storm. Now I have lost my way!"

"Are you a *real* princess?" asked the queen, eyeing the bedraggled girl with suspicion.

"Oh, yes, very much so, " answered the princess, "though I can hardly say I look like one right now."

The queen led the princess to a table next to a warm fire and brought her some food.

Now the queen had a son who had yet to marry. She did not want her son to marry just anyone. No, the prince must marry a real princess. But was this ragged girl to be believed? After a moment of thought, the queen had an idea. She would test the girl to see if she was a real princess. But how was this to be done?

"Of course, how simple!" shouted the queen, gleefully clapping her hands together.

"What did you say?" asked the princess, quite startled.

"Oh, never mind, child, never mind," said the queen. "You must be exhausted after being out in that storm. I will go and have your room made up at once." And the queen hurried upstairs.

"Quickly, quickly!" called the queen to her guard. "Gather twenty mattresses. Strip every other bedroom if you must. When you have them, place them in this room, one on top of the other. Then take a pea and place it on top of the bottommost mattress. Go now, be lively!"

The guard did as he was commanded, and with the prince's help stacked up all the mattresses. He then placed a pea under the next-to-the-last mattress.

"Good!" said the queen. "If this girl really is a princess, she will not be able to sleep the whole night long. Even through twenty mattresses a princess will feel the pea. Only a real princess is so sensitive!" Then she told the guard to bring the girl upstairs at once.

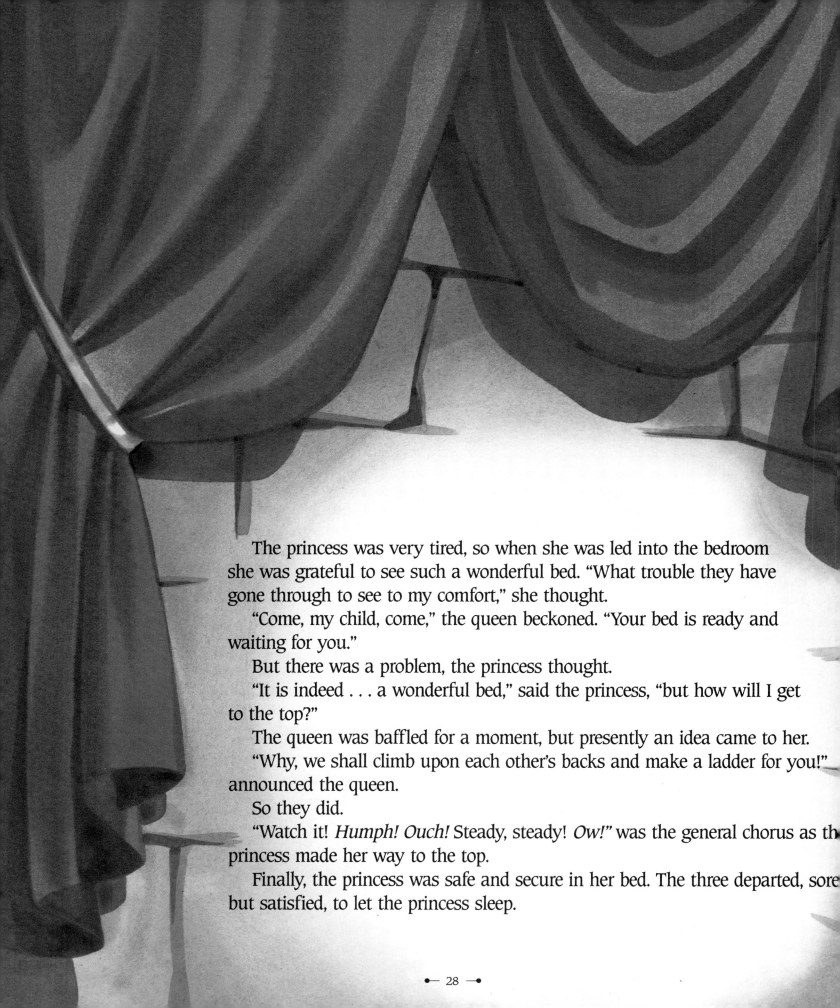

The princess was very tired, so when she was led into the bedroom she was grateful to see such a wonderful bed. "What trouble they have gone through to see to my comfort," she thought.

"Come, my child, come," the queen beckoned. "Your bed is ready and waiting for you."

But there was a problem, the princess thought.

"It is indeed . . . a wonderful bed," said the princess, "but how will I get to the top?"

The queen was baffled for a moment, but presently an idea came to her.

"Why, we shall climb upon each other's backs and make a ladder for you!" announced the queen.

So they did.

"Watch it! *Humph! Ouch!* Steady, steady! *Ow!*" was the general chorus as the princess made her way to the top.

Finally, the princess was safe and secure in her bed. The three departed, sore but satisfied, to let the princess sleep.

But the princess couldn't sleep.

Even with nineteen mattresses between her and the pea, she was in discomfort. She tossed and turned, and turned and tossed! She searched everywhere she could possibly think of for the source of her trouble, but without success.

The next morning, when the queen came to wake her, she found a thoroughly exhausted and miserable princess.

"How did you sleep, my dear?" asked the queen.

"I'm afraid I didn't sleep at all," said the princess with a long sigh. "Something horribly huge and lumpy was in my bed. No matter where I turned, it bruised me."

"You *are* a real princess," said the queen, happily.

The queen took the princess by the hand and led her downstairs, explaining how she had been tested to see if she was truly a real princess.

By this time the princess's coach had arrived at the castle.

"Now that I know you are a *real* princess," said the queen, "you can marry my son, the prince, and live happily ever after! Isn't that wonderful?"

"No, thank you," said the princess, rubbing her bruised back. "If this is the way you treat a guest, I shudder to think how you would treat a daughter-in-law! Goodbye!"

The princess stepped into her coach and was never seen in the kingdom again.

LITTLE BO-PEEP

Little Bo-Peep has lost her sheep,
And doesn't know where to find them;
Leave them alone, and they will come home,
Wagging their tails behind them.

LITTLE BOY BLUE

Little Boy Blue,
Come blow your horn!
The sheep's in the meadow,
The cow's is in the corn.
Where is the boy who looks
After the sheep?
He's under the haystack, fast asleep!

SING A SONG OF SIXPENCE

Sing a song of sixpence,
  A pocket full of rye,
Four and twenty blackbirds
  Baked in a pie!

When the pie was opened,
  The birds began to sing,
And wasn't that a dainty dish
  To set before the king?

MARY, MARY, QUITE CONTRARY

Mary, Mary, quite contrary,
  How does your garden grow?
With silver bells and cockle shells,
  And pretty maids all in a row.

HANSEL AND GRETEL

Beside a great forest lived a poor woodcutter with his wife and two children. The boy was named Hansel and the girl was named Gretel. Though, at times, life was very hard, they always had each other. For the woodcutter and his family that was all that mattered.

One morning the woodcutter had to go far into the forest to work, and would not return until the next day. His wife was also very busy mending chairs for the nearby villagers.

So Hansel and Gretel were left to play alone. And before long they had
wandered out of sight. They decided to go for a walk in the forest. Hansel
wanted to be careful not to get lost in the dark woods, so he brought along a
pocketful of bread crumbs. As they walked along, he dropped a few crumbs from
time to time, so that they were certain to find their way back home. But,
unknown to them, as they went deeper and deeper into the forest, a bird hopped
along behind them, eating every single crumb.

By the time Hansel realized what had happened, it was too late. Night was falling fast, and with little hope of finding their way out of the forest, they decided to lie down under the spreading branches of a large oak tree. As the last rays of light fled from the approaching night, Hansel and Gretel fell sound asleep.

Morning came and found the children rested but very hungry. They had not eaten since breakfast the day before. And other than a few wild berries, the forest had little food to offer the two children. They set off again through the woods, hoping to find their way back home. But, in fact, they were travelling deeper into the forest.

By mid-afternoon they had walked into the centre of the great woods. They soon came upon a small clearing. In the centre of this clearing stood a little cottage. But it was unlike any cottage they had seen before. Hansel and Gretel rubbed their eyes in disbelief. This cottage wasn't made of wood or stone. They looked again. Could it be true? It was true! This cottage was made of candy and cakes! With great excitement, the hungry children ran toward the little house.

How wonderful! The walls were made of
gingerbread and the roof was made with hard, sweet candies. And
everywhere were iced cakes, biscuits, and sweet dark chocolates. Why, even the
windowpanes were made of pure yummy sugar!

Hansel broke off a corner of a wall and happily nibbled the tasty morsels.
And Gretel munched on a piece of cupcake. Suddenly, there came a voice from
behind the cottage door. The voice was strangely musical, and sounded like
tinkling glass. It sang out:

"Nibbling, nibbling like a mouse,
who's that nibbling at my house?"

The door opened, and a very old woman came creeping out.

"Oh, you dear, sweet children!" she said. "Who has brought you here so far into the forest? Do come in, and stay with me. I'm just a lonely old woman who needs a little company. Come in, little ones, come in." She took both the smiling children by their hands, and led them into her little house.

The old woman was only pretending to be kind and gentle; she was really a wicked witch! She had built her candy cottage to entice little children to come near. When they did, she would invite them into her home where she would grab them and throw them into a cage. The wicked witch would then light her oven. For, you see, she liked to eat little children.

"Heh, heh, heh!" laughed the witch as she latched the cage, shutting Hansel and Gretel inside. "I have you now, and you'll not escape! My, what dainty dishes you shall make!" And she went at once to light her oven.

Hansel and Gretel were trapped, or so the witch thought. The witch busied herself at her oven, laughing and mumbling and singing to herself:

"Heh, heh, heh! A dinner of two.
My gingerbread house will always catch you!
You can run, yes! You can hide, oh!
But into my cooking pot, you shall go!"

"Heh, heh, heh, heh!" the witch had never been happier.

As the witch prepared her oven, she didn't pay the least bit of attention to Hansel and Gretel. And Hansel and Gretel paid no attention to her. They were still hungry. You see, the witch hadn't taken into account the appetites of little children, for Hansel and Gretel were the first children she had caught. So, Hansel and Gretel ate. They ate the cage, the table, the chairs, the cupboard, the cups, and—oh!—before long the entire cottage was gone and into their tummies!

"There, the oven is lit, and . . . oh! My beautiful home!" cried the
witch when she saw what had happened. "You naughty children! Look
at what you've done. My home, it's all gone! I slaved over the oven for
weeks to bake biscuits and sweets to build this house. Now, what will I do
to catch little children?"

The children just laughed, and Hansel let out a little burp.

"Enough!" screamed the witch, her face turning a bright red. "You are far
too much trouble. There must be something easier to eat than little children!"
The witch found her broomstick, one of the few things the children didn't eat,
and grabbed Hansel and Gretel. Then she climbed on the broomstick, crying out
in a shrill voice:

"Broomstick, broomstick, nickety-nack,
Obey my words, spit-a-dee, spat!
Fly over forest, fly over glen,
And send these children back home again!"

The broomstick did as it was commanded, flying them high above the great forest until they reached the children's home. The witch left Hansel and Gretel, safe and happy, in the loving arms of their parents. The witch flew off, and as she vanished from sight, she could clearly be heard to say:

"Hippety-hop, and nonsense talk
Of things that cannot be,
But know this is true, with children I'm through!
For they have driven me to P-O-V-E-R-T-Y!"

GEORGY PORGY

Georgy Porgy pudding and pie,
Kissed the girls and made them cry.
When the boys came out to play,
Georgy Porgy ran away.

OLD KING COLE

Old King Cole was a merry old soul,
And a merry old soul was he.
He called for his pipe,
He called for his bowl,
And he called for his fiddlers three!

RUB-A-DUB-DUB

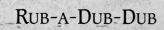

Rub-a-Dub-Dub,
Three men in a tub.
And who do you think they be?
The butcher,
The baker, the candlestick maker,
Terrible fools, all three.

JACK SPRAT

Jack Sprat could eat no fat,
His wife could eat no lean.
And so, between the two of them,
they licked the platter clean.

JACK AND THE BEANSTALK

There once was a poor widow who had a son named Jack. They lived in a small cottage not far from a little village. The winter had been very hard for them and, by spring, there was not a scrap of food left to eat.

"Come here, son," the mother called. Jack was a good and thoughtful boy, so he went at once to his mother's side. "We have nothing left to eat," the widow said with a sigh, "and we have no money to buy food. You will have to take Daisy to the village market and sell her—or we shall starve."

Daisy was their cow, and the family's last possession.

Jack reluctantly did as he was told. Placing a rope around Daisy's neck, he set off down the road with her toward the village market.

Along the way Jack met a very strange-looking man.

"My, my, my, just look at this fine cow you have," said the man. "I'll bet you're off to the market to sell her, eh? Good lad, but might I make you an offer, first?"

The man pulled from his pocket five little beans.

"Look close, my boy," the man began, "I will trade for this fine cow of yours these five magic beans." Then he sang:

"All of your wishes and most of your dreams,
Shall be granted to you by five little beans.
Life's many troubles strike weak and strong,
And trouble cares not for right or wrong.

"But if you are good, and if you are brave,
These five little beans will pave your way.
Take them, my boy, take them in hand,
Trust in the magic at your command!"

Jack happily swapped Daisy for the beans and hurried home to his mother.

"Back so soon, Jack?" asked his mother in amazement. "Well, I hope you got a good price for poor Daisy. Come, show me. How much money did she bring at the market?"

Jack proudly opened his hand to show his mother the five magic beans.

"What?! Beans?" cried Jack's mother. "You traded Daisy for a handful of beans?! How could you, Jack? Oh, my boy, what have you done? We shall surely starve now!" And she went inside the cottage to cry.

Jack had never felt more foolish. Magic beans, indeed! He was tempted to throw the horrid beans as far as he possibly could. But Jack thought better of it. At least the beans might give them something to eat this spring. He dug a little hole in the garden and dropped the beans in. Then he carefully covered them with dirt and watered them.

Ashamed, Jack went to his room and sobbed himself asleep.

The next morning, Jack rose early and went to greet the day at his window. Looking out, he could hardly believe his eyes. Where he had planted the five little beans there was now an enormous beanstalk! Enormous, why, it was the biggest and tallest beanstalk ever! It curled high above the cottage, up above the tallest mountain, and up through the clouds!

Jack wasted no time, and before his mother awoke, he quickly ran outside and began climbing the beanstalk. He knew now that the beans were magic, and that he must find out what was at the top of the beanstalk. He climbed, and climbed, and climbed! Before long, Jack was high above the valley and among the clouds. Still the beanstalk went higher!

When, at last, Jack reached the top of the beanstalk, he found himself in a strange and wonderful land. Glistening golden fields stretched out before him, ending at the edge of a dark and towering forest. Jack could see a colossal castle in the distance and wondered what kind of people lived in this land high above the clouds.

Jack made his way to the castle and, standing before its door, he realized that this castle was not just big, it was the biggest! The castle door was huge! It stood some thirty feet high, with a doorknob as large as he was. Jack gave a little shudder thinking of who lived in such a place. He took courage, though, remembering what the strange man had told him:

"If you are good, and if you are brave,
These five little beans will pave your way."

He squeezed himself under the door. Jack knew now that this land above the clouds was a land of giants.

Once inside, Jack made his way down a long hall and into an enormous dining room. In the dining room was a huge table, and on this table was food. Lots of food. The biggest-sized food Jack had seen in all his life! He decided at once to climb a leg of the table and gather as much food as possible to bring back to his poor mother. Jack had reached the top of the table when he felt it begin to shake and he heard what sounded like thunder. The sound grew louder and louder. Boom . . . Boom . . . Boom . . . BOOM!

Then he heard a deep voice say:

> "Fee-fie-fo-fum!
> I smell the blood of an Englishman.
> Be he alive, or be he dead,
> I'll grind his bones to make my bread."

Upon hearing this, Jack jumped into the sugar bowl to hide. Just in time, for at that moment a giant appeared. The giant had been busy all morning stealing cattle, tearing up crops, trampling on people's homes, and generally doing what giants like to do best. Needing a break from his work, he'd decided to come home to eat a giant meal and take a giant nap. But as soon as he entered the castle, his nostrils filled with a peculiar smell.

The giant looked everywhere, but he couldn't find Jack. Before long, the aroma of dinner overwhelmed the giant's attention, and he sat down to eat. When he was through with his meal, the giant took down his two most prized posessions: a hen that laid golden eggs and a beautiful harp that sang with the voice of an angel. The giant commanded the hen to lay three golden eggs. One, two, three golden eggs appeared. Pleased with the hen, the giant then commanded the harp to sing as he settled down for a nap. He soon fell fast asleep to the gentle voice of the harp. With the giant asleep, Jack crept out of the sugar bowl and tiptoed across the table.

Suddenly it occurred to him that he would not need to steal food if he had a hen that laid golden eggs. Reaching the hen, Jack grabbed her and began to make his way to the edge of the table. Just before he started to climb down, the harp sang out to him:

"Brave boy, brave boy, don't leave without me,
A prisoner I am of the giant you see.
Take me away from this ogre with you,
And I'll sing pretty tunes all your days through."

Jack was about to return for the harp when the giant began to stir. He quickly hid behind the bowl of fruit. The giant said sleepily:

"Fee-fie-fo-fum!
I smell the blood . . . ahhhh! . . . of an Englishman."
The giant rubbed his eyes a bit
and cleared his throat.
"Be he alive or be he dead,
I'll grind his bones to make my bread.
Hee, hee, oh yes, yes, I will, I surely will."

The giant fell back asleep.

Jack acted quickly, and running back across the table, he scooped the harp up under one arm, as he held the hen tightly under the other. He had almost made it to the edge of the table when he slipped on a pat of butter. The harp cried out as they fell, and the giant awoke. Without losing his grip on either hen or harp, Jack jumped from the table and ran for the door.

"I knew it! I knew it!" the giant cried in anger. "You won't escape me, little man." And the giant began to chase after Jack.

Jack made it safely to the beanstalk, but only because the giant tripped twice over his own huge feet. With the hen on his head and the harp under one arm, Jack began to climb down the beanstalk. The giant, peered down through the clouds, and seeing Jack, began to climb down after him.

Jack reached the bottom ahead of the giant, but with huge strides the giant was only moments away from overtaking him. Jack quickly set the hen and harp down and grabbed an axe. When his mother ran from the cottage to greet him, she let out a cry as she saw the giant lumbering down upon them.

Jack chopped away at the beanstalk with all his might, until he cut it clean in two. The stalk gave way and came crashing down.

"Oh, noooooo!" screamed the giant as he covered his eyes, facing a nasty fall to earth.

But luckily for the giant, the beanstalk fell out over the nearby sea. No one knew if he could swim, but the giant was never seen again.

Jack, his mother, the hen, and the harp lived a very long and happy life together.

THE END

The Flintstones® is a registered trademark of
Hanna-Barbera Productions, Inc.
Copyright © 1994 by Turner Publishing, Inc.
All Rights Reserved.
Published by Bedrock Press
1050 Techwood Drive, N.W., Atlanta, GA 30318
ISBN: 1-57036-021-9
First Edition 10 9 8 7 6 5 4 3 2 1
Distributed by Pegasus Sales and Distribution Limited
Unit 5B, Causeway Park, Wilderspool Causeway,
Warrington, Cheshire WA4 6QE

Designed and Illustrated by VACCARRO ASSOCIATES INC.
Layouts by BOB SINGER Painted by DENNIS DURRELL
Additional Design/Layouts: HAMID ROSTAMIAN/ROGER A. ESTRADA
Production Management: JON I. ROSENBERG